The Crystal Journey Adventures

Book 1

Mermaid City

by
Deni Bressette

Illustrations by
Jason Altice

Copyright © 2015 Deni Bressette.

All rights reserved. No part of this book may be used or reproduced by any means, graphic, electronic, or mechanical, including photocopying, recording, taping or by any information storage retrieval system without the written permission of the author except in the case of brief quotations embodied in critical articles and reviews.

Balboa Press books may be ordered through booksellers or by contacting:

Balboa Press
A Division of Hay House
1663 Liberty Drive
Bloomington, IN 47403
www.balboapress.com
1 (877) 407-4847

Because of the dynamic nature of the Internet, any web addresses or links contained in this book may have changed since publication and may no longer be valid. The views expressed in this work are solely those of the author and do not necessarily reflect the views of the publisher, and the publisher hereby disclaims any responsibility for them.

Any people depicted in stock imagery provided by Thinkstock are models, and such images are being used for illustrative purposes only. Certain stock imagery © Thinkstock.

ISBN: 978-1-5043-4512-5 (sc)
ISBN: 978-1-5043-4513-2 (e)

Library of Congress Control Number: 2015918943

Print information available on the last page.

Balboa Press rev. date: 12/15/2015

Dedication

I thank my grandchildren for inspiring their De De to begin an imaginative, empowering series for young readers. Zac, Simone, Fiona, Stella, and Ledger Fox….you munchkins are my heart!

Readers will recognize these names as each book publishes, since they are all characters in one form or fashion!

Prologue

Simone could barely sleep as her mind raced. This could be one of the most important moments of her entire life. She had made a discovery, one she thought completely impossible.

She had discovered how to swim with the mermaids. And, it was all quite by accident.

The thing of it is, when she attempted this newfound secret by herself, she found it was much too scary to travel into her daydreams all alone.

If she could just convince her dog, Coop, to go with her, everything would be fine. Convincing him might be a different story since he was scared of *everything, including his own shadow*. But, if they were going to do it, the time was now.

Tonight, they would attempt her biggest daydream ever. If there was anything in the world Simone wanted, it was to frolic and learn from the mermaids. She thought they were beautiful, smart and oh, so wise.

Excitement ran through her body at the thought of journeying under the sea to swim with the mermaids.

Chapter One

Lying in her bed, Simone petted her sleeping dog, Coop. His head was laying on her legs, and his huge body took up most of the bed.

"I've decided that we need to go on an adventure together. We are going to travel under the ocean and swim with mermaids. What do you think about that, buddy?"

He did not even bother to lift his head but, instead, ignored her. He hoped she would go to sleep and forget this crazy thinking. A mermaid? *How about a sea dragon*, he thought as he closed his eyes and began to snore.

Oblivious to his slumbering state, Simone continued to ramble on. "It's a good thing Mom taught me how to meditate, otherwise I would never have figured out how to travel to the mermaids. Mom said meditating would quiet my mind, and because of that, it would help me imagine things in my mind much easier. If it really works, we should all try it. "We could have a class, and you could be in it too," she said to her favorite stuffed fox she had named 'Wizard.' He simply stared back at her.

"You know, Wizard, the other day when I meditated with Mom, my mind took me to a little beach cove. I saw *you,* as a grown fox. You were dressed in clothes and *talked*."

He appeared to grin, as if he knew exactly what she was talking about.

"Wizard, you told me I could travel into any daydream I wanted. I've decided I want to swim with mermaids. I imagined it while I meditated, and it scared me to think of going all by myself, but if Coop comes with me, I won't be afraid."

Mom peeked her head in the door. "Go to sleep, sweetie. Even though it's summer that doesn't mean you don't need to rest."

"Okay, night Mom. I will lay down in one minute," she said as she blew her mom a kiss.

Simone smiled to herself. "It's summer all right, and I'm going on vacation tonight. Under the ocean and wearing mermaid tails for us, Coop!"

She pulled her ancient mermaid language book out from under her pillow and began to read out loud. She felt pretty proficient at mermaid language since she practiced every day.

"Are you ready to *'pron'* with the *'tessas shorane'*? That means swim with the mermaids forever in ancient mermaid language!"

Tucking her book into her pocket, she was excited now as she shook his body to wake him up. "Come on, we better try this out tonight while everyone else is asleep and won't notice we are gone. Give me your paw, Coop, and let's begin."

Disgruntled at being woken up, he unwillingly handed her his paw. He was thinking that this fantasy could not possibly turn out well for him. His heart was beating loudly as he listened to her whispering voice.

"Let's take three big breaths, so we won't be nervous. Breathe in through your nose, Coop, and then out of your mouth like you are fogging a mirror." She demonstrated the breathing for him so he would copy her.

Coop's snores filled the room. "Not that kind of breathing, goof. Wake up and breathe with me and don't fall asleep again. Now, take another deep breath, close your eyes, and pretend we are walking along the beach. Keep your eyes closed, Coop. This is very important so that we see the same thing and travel to the same place."

The room was very silent, except for the sound of Simone and Coop breathing.

Chapter Two

There was a light, shooting sparks through the night like a fireworks show. The light was actually a tunnel surrounded by a beautiful rainbow. The rainbow had seven beautiful colors glowing through the sky above the tunnel. Red, orange, yellow, green, turquoise, blue and purple lit up the darkness.

Coop thought, *I think I'll open my eyes because I am not sure if I want to see what will happen when the tunnel reaches us.* But, he remembered it was important to keep them closed.

They heard the tunnel gently hit land, and then the door slowly began to open.

What if it was an alien space ship coming to take them away? Coop thought to himself as he almost decided to jump off the bed.

Suddenly, out jumped a red fox!

"Wizard! Is that really you? You look so different!" Simone exclaimed when her stuffed animal stood before her.

"Ha! Bet you are happy to see me."

She truly was glad to see him standing there. He stood taller than her, on his back two feet. His red hair was spiked straight up like a rock star, and he was wearing a blue velvet jacket adorned with silver moons and stars. He held a wooden staff that had been carved into a fox head at the top.

The fox quickly corrected her. "On this journey, I am a magical Wizard, and I am about to take you right into your daydream."

"You can really take us under the ocean in this tunnel? You know all I ever daydream about is swimming with the mermaids."

"Well, once I engage my crystal ball," said Wizard, you can choose wherever you want to go. But, first. What's with the dog cowering behind you?" Wizard looked at Coop as if he were completely ridiculous.

"He is my best friend and travel companion. He will protect me wherever we go," Simone said as she pulled Coop toward the tunnel.

Shaking his head, Wizard thought out loud. "What a pathetic protector this mutt will be. But, if you insist on bringing him, that's up to you. Now, leave your shoes by the door and tip-toe into my sacred tunnel, please."

"Come on, Coop. Get in here." It was not easy for a ten-year-old girl to pull a one hundred forty pound great dane. Finally, she pulled him through the door.

"Whew," as she fell backward into the tunnel. "Come on, buddy. This will be fun."

They walked quietly through the dimly lit space. She had so many questions. "Why is there a rainbow around this lighted tunnel?"

Tapping his staff twice on the floor, Wizard danced a little jig. "That is the tunnel's protection bubble. Keeps us out of harm's way and safe. Good thing to do, Missy, even around our own bodies."

As Wizard tapped the glowing wall with his staff, a huge worn map began to unroll from the ceiling. "Where do you and your dog want to travel?"

"All I want to do is swim with the mermaids. Can we go where they live?" Simone played nervously with the little moonstone owl necklace she always wore around her neck on a turquoise ribbon. Her grandmother had given it to her for her tenth birthday that year and she wore it for protection.

The map showed many different islands scattered throughout the vast ocean. Mumbling to himself, Wizard ran his pointer claw over the map. "Voila! Mermaid Island it is," he said as he slapped the piece of land with his paw.

Simone jumped up and down as she clapped her hands. "There really is a place to swim with mermaids. I can't wait! Can we go now, Wizard?"

Chapter Three

Snap! His fingers produced a clear crystal the size of a baseball. He held it in his left paw, while he rubbed it with his right. Closing his eyes, he began to chant, "Show me the way to Mermaid Island."

Suddenly, long strips of purple lightning flashed from his paw, and the tunnel began to move. Slowly at first, and then....... *whoosh!!!!*

He threw his head back in laughter, and began his peculiar little jig again. "Don't be scared, you two. This is going to be the smoothest ride of your life, but you better hold on!"

"Ruff, Ruff, Ruff," screeched Coop. His eyes were the size of saucers, his ears blown back behind his head. He was terrified, and he didn't care who knew it. Poor Coop.

"Coop, close your mouth and stop screaming. You have slobber hanging all the way back to your shoulder, and it's disgusting," said Simone. His eyes simply grew larger, drool longer, ears floppier.

Wizard's hair was standing straight up, and it made Simone think she understood the crazy hairdo now. *This is probably what it would be like walking through a tornado or a windstorm,* she thought.

Twirling her hair in anticipation, she wondered what the island would be like. Would they really see mermaids? Would they be able to breathe?

"Full Moon out there," Wizard shouted above the noisy wind. "Makes for the best time to travel for magic." His feet did the little dance again.

"You know, they say fox is called upon for quick thinking and blending in to your surroundings instead of standing out. I would say you will need these attributes for your journey. You will be very different amongst the sea life."

He tapped the floor with his staff, and looked very serious. "There is a very important rule you must follow in this daydream. If you do not follow it, you will never be allowed to travel through the tunnel again. Do you understand?"

Simone reached for Coop's paw and held it in her hand. "We promise to follow your rules, Wizard. We want to travel a lot, don't we Coop?"

Oh, yeah, sure. All the time, he thought, hoping his dinner did not come up.

"You must return home before daylight. We never want your parents to be afraid or worried because you are not where you are supposed to be. This is a rule you must follow at home as well."

"We promise," said Simone as she crossed her heart.

"Approaching land, I see. Look below, it is your island. This tunnel is going to begin descending under the ocean, so put your tunnel belt on!"

Simone felt like she was going to throw up. She knew it must be nerves and fear combined. "Under the water? How will we breathe, or talk? What if we drown? Oh, I think I want you to take us home now, Wizard."

"Have you forgotten? This is magic. We can do anything we want in this daydream. You will be just fine." Wizard patted her head. "Follow me to the front of the tunnel, and we will prepare for exit."

The closer to the front of the tunnel they got, the more it started to change in looks. Glowing white walls were now crystal-studded and sparkling with purples, blues, whites, pinks, emerald, turquoise, black, and every other color she could imagine. It was gorgeous.

Even more excited now, she jumped back when the purple lightning streaks glowed from Wizard's paws, and she watched him pluck a black stone from its bed in the wall.

Wizard turned to Coop, wearing a very serious expression on his face. "Now listen up. This Black Tourmaline stone will fill you with courage and strength to be Simone's brave protector on this journey, as well as journeys to come. You will notice your fear gradually residing, then suddenly brave takes over!"

Purple flashed from the fox's paws and directed the black stone right into Coop's blue leather collar.

Turning again, he plucked another stone from the wall, this time a purple one. "This is an Amethyst and it will give you a strong voice in any situation that comes. Both stones will protect you."

Chapter Four

Zap!

Coop jumped when the crystal embedded itself next to the black stone, and the weirdest thing happened. His muscles became very strong, as his head grew bigger and his body taller.

"Don't look so shocked, strange dog. Soon, you will be fearless and powerful. Now, if you ever need me, rub this purple stone with your paw, and I will instantly appear. If I need you to return to me immediately, your black stone will flash on and off. Get it?"

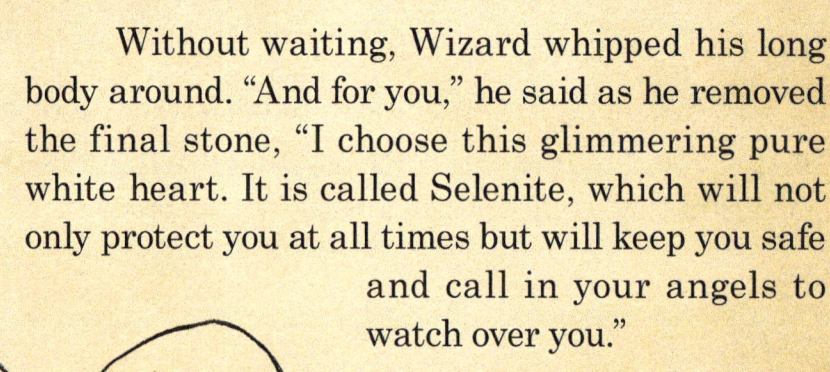

Without waiting, Wizard whipped his long body around. "And for you," he said as he removed the final stone, "I choose this glimmering pure white heart. It is called Selenite, which will not only protect you at all times but will keep you safe and call in your angels to watch over you."

The heart fit perfectly in her hands. "It's beautiful, Wizard. Thank you so much."

"Remember to always listen to your intuition. You know that weird feeling you get in your tummy, known as 'gut feeling?' That is what you always pay attention too.

Both of you. And, Simone, if you need me, rub the heart between your hands and I will appear."

He opened the tunnel door. "Time to go."

He laid the palm of his paw on Coop's forehead. "There is nothing wrong with being afraid. We all get scared at times. But, when you make yourself feel brave, you *become* brave. You are never going to be the same from this moment on."

Once again, his paw flashed. "Please open your mouth, Coop," Wizard said.

Coop opened his mouth as if he were about to yawn. "I'll try not to be scared. I will be Coop, the Wonder Dog!" *Oh no, what have I gotten myself into*, he thought.

"You talked, you talked!" Simone clapped her hands as she danced around in glee. "This makes it real, we are really going into my daydream together."

Wizard raised his hand over his head. "Ok, enough, now go. Remember, you must be back before dawn."

Coop and Simone held hand and paw as they faced the opening. Grinning at each other, they barely heard Wizard yelling "One, Two, Three, Jump," as they hurtled right into her daydream.

Everything was silent. There was no movement, no bubbles, no noise, nothing as they sunk deeper and deeper into the eerie dark ocean. It was very hard to see as they swam along holding on to one another for dear life.

Eventually, light began to filter through the water, and it was soon clear as glass. Looking over her shoulder, Simone watched Coop's body swim through the water.

Something looked different, something besides the bigger body that came with his stones. She stared harder.

"Coop, you have wings and a dorsal fin on your back! You're huge!"

He looked down at his body and yelped. "Ahhh, my body is powerful! You didn't know it, but the whole time you daydreamed of swimming with mermaids, I dreamed of becoming a sea dragon. This is exactly how I imagined it," he said as he tipped back and forth through the water.

"Coop, you are funny. I feel like I'm on a see-saw. It might take you awhile to get used to these huge wings of yours. You sure don't seem as scared as I thought you would be."

The silver wings glittered in the sunlight, as he proudly spread them wide. They were gleaming as he swam through the water.

"Hold on tight, here we go," he said as he attempted flips and dives in the water. He did not want her to see how nervous he was with his new responsibilities. It was quite different being her guard here in a strange environment. *What if I can't do this. What if I can't protect her. What if I am too scared of all these strange animals under the water?* he thought nervously. *You must make yourself be brave*, he repeated Wizard's words to himself.

Chapter Five

They dodged a swarm of jellyfish and came upon a whale shark and her pup. They were both completely speechless as they stared in awe at the creature moving toward them through the water.

"Look, Mommy, a human and a sea dragon," said the pup. "Are you lost?" he asked Simone and Coop.

"Indeed, are you lost?" asked the mother as she glided up behind her baby.

"We are looking for Mermaid City," Simone stuttered. She grinned, realizing this was really happening.

"Go straight ahead towards the sun, turn left at the kelp forest, and follow the coral reef. You will see signs to the cove."

"Hey, Mommy, do you think we can give them a ride?" Mother laughed and said, "I think they will be just fine, unless they want company."

Finally finding his voice, Coop said, "We're okay, but thank you." He hoped they would not notice his wings were quivering in fear.

As they parted ways, dragon and girl swam along in silence, each lost in thought.

"That would have been too weird traveling with the largest fish in the sea, let alone a *shark*," said Coop. *And way too scary,* he thought. *That was a little too close for comfort.*

"Actually Coop, scientists call whale sharks gentle giants." Simone said. "They eat microscopic animals called plankton, not humans."

"You know everything, Simone." His face was filled with adoration for her.

"Well, it kinda helps having a marine scientist for a mom," she said.

After following the whale shark's directions, they finally arrived at a cove. They were greeted by six colorful seahorses.

"Welcome to Mermaid Cove," they sang in unison. "You may only enter the city if you know the secret password."

"Secret password?" yelped and Coop.

Simone and Coop looked at each other and he shrugged his big shoulders. "Can you give us a hint?" he asked the seahorses.

"Well, if you know anything about mermaids, you should be able to figure this out," they replied.

Feeling defensive, Simone says, "I know *a lot* about mermaids."

The seahorses laugh. "It's not that easy. It's a lot more ancient than that."

Simone racked her brain, and thought about all the mermaid books she had read, but her mind was drawing a blank.

"What about your ancient mermaid language book," Coop whispered. "Yes!" She hugged him tight with one hand, and yanked the book out of her back pocket. "*Turon, Orora, Hortume*!" Each time the seahorses giggled. "Nope. Try again."

Her eyes began to well up with tears. "We've come so far, we can't give up now. How will we ever guess this stupid password, Coop?"

Coop said, "Your Selenite heart. Remember Wizard said if you need help to reach for your stone?"

"You're a genius!" Simone exclaimed.

Coop clapped his wings and blushed as he watched her cup the heart in her hand. She closed her eyes, and took a deep breath. *I must be strong for her,* he thought nervously.

Words and images flashed through her mind, but nothing felt right, until........"*Sessa!*" she screamed. "It's the ancient Atlantis name for mermaids!"

The seahorses jumped and began to dance, "Brilliant! Your stone must be magic! You may now enter the secret city." Gracefully, they bowed their heads and moved aside, as they watched Simone and Coop enter Mermaid City.

Chapter Six

Sparkly jellyfish floated along the path, lighting the way for them as they walked through the entrance. It was very noisy as different type of sea life hustled down the path to one destination or another.

"This sure is an active city," commented Simone just as a large Ladyfish bumped into her. She was carrying a polkadot umbrella, and her lips were pursed in annoyance as she hustled by. "Excuse me," she mumbled, without giving them a second glance.

A chorus of singing fish rode by atop a large yellow crab. Coop's eyebrows raised. He was perplexed as to why the crab was carrying a bunch of singing fish on his back. "That is the weirdest looking thing I've ever seen," he said to Simone.

A bystander swam up to where they were floating. "Excuse me, that's not just *any* crab. He is Diego the Decorator crab, and the reason he camouflaged himself in yellow seaweed is because he is our local school bus.

"Oh, that is so cool! Look at his arm stuck out to the side with the stop sign! I love it here," laughed Simone.

There was a sudden hush on the busy path, as pedestrians began to scurry to the side. Diego the Decorator crab swooped Simone and Coop up with his claw. "Sit here on the bus, you will be safer. No telling what she would do with strange looking fish like you."

"Who? What's going on?" Simone was confused by the sudden nervous behavior. Coop pointed and said "Look."

Simone gasped when she saw the line of mermaids carrying a very big conch shell on a stretcher. There must have been at least ten of them swimming along. "Why is that shell on an ambulance stretcher?"

Crab's eye rolled back to look at her. "That's called a litter, and they are carrying the Queen to her kingdom. If you look ahead, you can see it in the distance."

Simone shivered when she saw the huge, foreboding sand castle tucked back amongst rocks and darkness. There was a thick brown seaweed fence surrounding it, with tall gates that appeared to be very big shark teeth. Sharks surrounded the outside entrance, snapping their strong jaws every few seconds.

"I don't think anyone very nice lives there," said Coop. *And I don't feel afraid of this, that's a shocker,* although he kept that thought to himself.

There was absolute silence as the crowd watched the

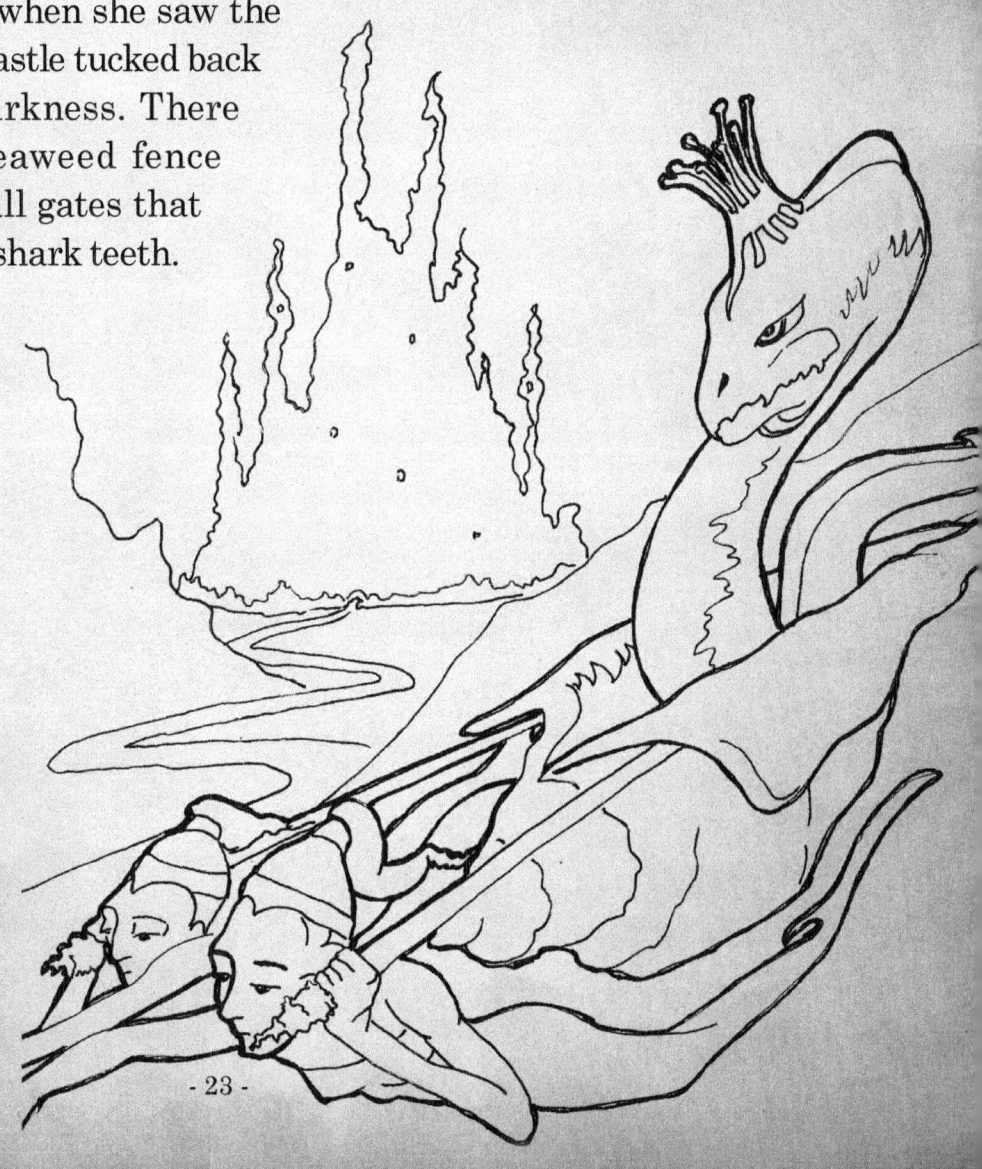

Queen pass by. She wore a scowl on her face and stared straight ahead, yelling orders to the poor mermaids carrying her.

"Scrunch down," whispered Diego. "You don't want her to see you."

As they sunk deeper into the yellow seaweed, Simone watched sadly and thought about how unhappy the mermaids looked. "I wish we could help them," she whispered in Coop's ear.

"There's nothing anyone can do," Diego said sadly. "She is the meanest queen alive."

Once the caravan was safely out of sight, Simone and Coop hopped off the crab's back and waved goodbye, and began to swim away. They were eager to see the rest of the city, but conscious to stay away from the castle.

A short way up the path, they came upon a sea cave with a rickety driftwood sign that read 'Shark Bait Tavern.'

"Do you think we should go in?" she asked Coop.

Two huge grouper fish guard the door. "I don't know," he replied. *Those fish*

look awfully big, he thought. Coop hoped he would be able to feel as strong as he acted. *After all*, he thought, *I have Black Tourmaline and Amethyst to help me.*

"What do you two want?" barked one of the guards, as he uncrossed his fins from his chest.

"We are new in town and would like to visit the cave," said Coop.

One of the grouper snorted and blew a stream of bubbles from his mouth. "Yeah? The price to get in here is a chunk of meat for both of us. Otherwise, keep on swimming."

Coop snapped his paw, producing two nice chunks of meat. "Here you go," he said, wearing a lopsided grin as he looked at a shocked Simone.

"Go on in," smacked the groupers happily.

"How in the world did you do that?" Simone asked. "I have no idea. I just imagined they were there, and they were! I also found I did not really fear those guards, either. Maybe my crystals are working!" Coop responded.

The cave was dim. "It looks like we are in a restaurant," Simone said. There were massive laughing shrimp leaning against a tall table, and sharks played a game that used sticks to knock balls around a table.

Surveying the room, Coop did not like what he saw. "Let's go. There's nothing but trouble here. Besides we don't want to be shark bait." He felt a new strength brewing inside his body as he realized it might be time to protect his girl.

"Where do you think you are going?" said a group of scraggly looking fish with nipped fins.

The shark with the rusty hook piercing in his lip puffed his chest and moved toward them. "We are the shark patrol. Did you really think you could come in here and leave alive?"

Just as Simone thought about swimming out the door, Coop reared up on his hind legs, took a deep breath, and yelled, "BOO." Hot flames came out of his mouth, and the sharks scattered like terrified sand fleas.

"My gut says it's time to go, so give me your hand, Simone." They swam as fast as they could to the street.

"Those sharks were wimps when they saw that fire come out of your mouth." gasped Simone. Coop thought the same thing. "Yeah, but I still don't want to cross their paths again. Hop on my back, girl." He was feeling stronger all the time; his fear was beginning to disappear as they swam deeper into the Mermaid City.

They meandered slowly along the path, and were both quiet as they took in their surroundings. A colorful lion fish was mowing his seagrass, while a clown fish playfully darted in and out of the anemones.

Things were pretty quiet, and just as they talked about resting, they came to another cave. This one was tucked back, well off the path. Little did they know, this cave held all the magic they sought.

Chapter Seven

The sign was surrounded in shimmering seaweed and read 'The School of Mermaids.' There were huge aqua crystals lining the entranceway, and jutting up from the ocean floor, all like stars.

Dolphin calves swam circles around them as Coop reached the entrance. They wore little purple tank tops that read 'Mermaids have more fun.'

"Hi, Dolphins, I think mermaids would have more fun, too. Is this really a school?" said Simone.

The calves made clicking sounds as they performed flips. "Why, yes it is. Welcome to mermaid school," they whistled together.

An older dolphin swam up to Simone and Coop. He wore little round spectacles on his bottle shaped nose and a black bow-tie around his neck. "Yes, this is a school. Can I help you?"

"Well, we would like to attend this school if it teaches us how to become a mermaid," said Simone.

"So, you want to be a mermaid, do you," he asked quizically. "Why?"

"Well, I have always wanted to swim with the mermaids, but if I could become one, I would be able to breathe underwater all the time, and I would be one with the sea animals."

"There is a lot more to being a mermaid than just those things," the older dolphin replied. "My name is Mr. Flip, and I am the principal of the school. Let's go meet the head mermaid and she can decide if you attend."

"Decide? But I already know I'd be a great mermaid."

"Well, you are human and this school only teaches sea life," Mr. Flip said as he nudged the door open with his nose. "The dragon needs to swim low. We don't want our ceiling crystals broken."

They swam through the entrance. It was very quiet. The walls were lined with sea life behavior manuals and language dictionaries. Clamshells tucked in-between the shelves, appear to be study desks.

They came upon a room filled with huge shells nestled in the sand. "Those look like conch shells my Mom and I find on the beach. If you hold it to your ear, it sounds like the ocean, but only if there is no crab inside."

Mr. Flip whistled. "These are different conch shells. In Mermaid's Cove, they house sea sprites. The sprites help make the shells and then give them to hermit crabs."

The sprites had beautiful blue wings, double their body size, and were sparkling with crystals. The tiny creatures danced one by one across the shells, moving toward Simone.

They began to sing and spin right in front of her feet *"We are about to graduate from sea sprite school! When a nice Queen moves into the Kingdom, we will get to move in and take care of her sea plants and flowers."*

"Would all of you get to go to the kingdom?"

"Yes, we will one day. We will also get to help guard the crystal cave formations from being chipped or ruined. Why are you here? You look very strange," said the sprite as she looked Coop and Simone over. They all began to snicker.

"We have to study now, but please come visit us again! Bye!" said the sprites as they twirled off happily back to the shells.

Mr. Flip seems to enjoy the sprites immensely. "They are such a joy while here at school. The new Queen will be fortunate enough to have them until their twenty-fifth birthday. If we ever *get* a new Queen, that is. They would not be safe in the kingdom with the present situation, so we keep the sprites busy here in hopes things will change."

"Yes, we saw the mean Queen. I would never want to be in that castle with her. What happens when the sprites turn twenty-five?" Simone was completely intrigued.

"At that time, they rise to the top of the water, drop hundreds of tiny eggs that sink to the bottom of the ocean, and the cycle begins all over again. The parents become dragonflies that skim through the sky and oversee the land. They are very special."

Splash!

Coop leaped into the circle of sea sprites, who were zipping playfully around his head. He was wild with puppy-like excitement and for a moment forgot he was a scared sea dragon trying very hard to be brave.

Clapping his fins together, Mr. Flip clicked loudly to the mischievous sprites. "Play time is up. Get busy with your studies now, sprites!" Turning to Simone, he said, "We need to move along now as well, and you must make a very important decision, one you may not like too well."

"If you are allowed in school, what do you plan to do with your dragon?"

"What do you mean? Coop must come to school with me, because he is my best friend and protector," Simone insisted.

Coop grins as he swam along behind. "I am her protector. I go where she goes," he said as he flaps his wings for emphasis. *I don't feel very scared at that thought anymore*, he thought.

"Well, we shall see, dragon. But don't be surprised if you are not allowed in. Now, follow me through the glass door right ahead," said Mr. Flip.

Chapter Eight

Determined not to worry about the situation, Simone followed the dolphin through a door etched with a beautiful mermaid. The wonderland on the other side was breathtaking.

Sea turtle babies floated slowly along, bobbing up and down gently. Chubby baby octopus were frolicking through the water alongside their Father, and baby seahorses rode along on the backs of their mothers. *It is peaceful and amazing*, Simone thought.

Simone really missed her mom at that moment. She thought about how much she would enjoy being free to swim and breathe with the sea life. Maybe they could come here together one day.

The silence was broken with a loud scuffle. "Aarggh, get off me," huffed Coop.

Swimming quickly to the end of a hall, Simone saw what the ruckus was all about. She burst out laughing when she saw a bunch of baby octopus legs dangling down Coop's head. Their little round bodies bounced up and down as they squealed, "Giddyap, horsey, giddyap!"

"Stop laughing and get these things out of my nose!" Coop was desperately trying to wriggle free from the sticky tentacles, although he was actually happy to have found some sea creatures who liked him.

Suddenly, a shrill whistle echoed off the cave walls. Mr. Flip hustled over to the chaos. "Omar, Olly, Osteen, Opal, get off that dragon, *neeooowwwwwww!* Get back to Octopus Cove or you will be grounded for a week!"

They were pouting as they slid off Coop's head and back but only because they did not want to be in time out. Filing out of the cave, Olly threw Coop a dirty look.

"Sorry, please don't be mad at me. I would have played with you," Coop mumbled. He felt sad to see them go. He finally felt like he had made some friends.

Olly looked over his shoulder and winked. "Okay. Maybe I'll see you sometime soon!"

"Almost there. Soon I must leave you and return to my desk to carry out principal duties." Smiling, Mr. Flip motioned them ahead with his fin.

Finally, we are almost there, Simone thought to herself as her tummy flipped in excitement.

An orangey colored starfish surrounded Simone and Coop as they approached the classroom. The starfish gently moved across their bodies, examining them inch by inch. "You don't look like normal students who come here. Are you human?" asked one of the two largest seastars in the group.

Simone giggled as she spread her hand so the star would rest in her palm. "I am human, but I want to be a mermaid. This is my pet dragon."

She noticed this starfish had twelve shorter arms circled in bands of yellow and red. Its body was covered with small spines that looked like a magnificent sun.

The star fish lifted one of her arms and pointed at Coop. "He wants to become a mermaid? That would be pretty funny."

"Not a mermaid," Coop quickly corrected. "I am just visiting."

"Don't be so sure," the starfish giggled. "There's no telling what that Queen will do to you. She is not very nice to sea life. I can't even imagine what she would do with humans. Beware!"

A black chalkboard covered the full length of one wall. 'Welcome to Mermaid School. Teacher: Miss Meranda. Please be seated' was written in turquoise calligraphy handwriting.

Open clamshells, big enough for chairs, dotted the floor of the classroom. Other students were already seated, as they waited for the teacher to arrive.

Hopping into an oversized clamshell, Simone thought it felt pretty comfortable for being a hard shell. She patted the chair next to her, and motioned for Coop. "Come sit down next to me. These are all sea creatures in here. I feel kinda weird, don't you?"

"Yes, I don't think we fit in here," he said as he backed up to the clamshell. Just as his bottom reached the edge of the clamshell, it flew out from beneath him, skimming across the room like a frisbee in mid-air.

He was mortified! And, just as he thought things could not get any worse, the flying chair completed a circle, and began moving directly toward his head!

Chapter Nine

Whack!

The flying chair hit right against his dragon head. Laughter filled the room, but Coop quickly decided to turn the tables. He stood up tall, bent at his waist, and bowed to the students. "Glad you enjoyed the show," he grinned as he pranced around the classroom, feeling quite proud of himself.

The laughter abruptly stopped. There was complete silence in the room except for the creaky chalkboard rolling up toward the ceiling.

Swish, swish, swish. It sounded like fish swimming to and fro, but instead of fish…..it was a ………..

She moved quietly into the room. Blonde hair flowed freely around her as her arms swayed daintily at her side. Her magnificent blue eyes were big and round, surrounded by thick, dark lashes; her skin appeared to be smooth as silk.

Every single creature in the room was star struck as the magnificent emerald tail sparkled across the room. The mermaid smiled at each student as she passed by.

Simone was beside herself. *I can't believe this is happening*, she thought, as she fought the urge to pinch herself. Coop's head nodded back and forth, eyes wide as saucers.

When the Mermaid spoke, her voice sounded like a sweet songbird. "Hello students, and welcome to class orientation. I am Miss Meranda, Head Teacher of the school. "And now, we are going around the room to introduce ourselves. Please give me your name, where you are from, and why you want to become a mermaid."

She listened patiently as students shared their desire to live in the mermaid kingdom with the Queen. Most thought it was easy to become a mermaid, especially since they were already sea animals.

Finally!

Simone twisted her hair madly around her finger, thankful for her turn. She could not believe that she was actually speaking to a live mermaid.

"My name is Simone, and I live on the land. Our house is on the beach, though. I have always dreamed of swimming with mermaids."

Taking a deep breath for courage, she continued. "You see, I have learned how to travel into my favorite daydream. I would love to take this class, so I can come back anytime and be of great service to the sea population."

"A daydream? Well, that would mean we weren't real, if it were a daydream, and we are indeed very real," Miss Meranda said with a reassuring smile. And, who might this odd creature be sitting next to you?"

Using his mammoth wings to push himself from the low chair, he stood up proudly. His courage surfaced, his fears slipped away. "My name is Coop, and I am a magical sea dragon in this daydream. My job here is to protect my girl. I don't want to be a mermaid."

"Ah, I see," the teacher said as she tapped her chin with her pointer finger. "And, just what exactly is wrong with being a mermaid?"

"Arrrooofff, nothing. I'm a dragon in this daydream, not a fish, but when I am on land, I am what the humans call a Great Dane," he said proudly.

"So, does that make you head of the dog kingdom?"

Nodding his head vigorously up and down, he avoided eye contact with Simone. "Yes, I am king dog on land!"

Swimming between the chairs, Miss Meranda continued to speak in her soft, gentle voice.

"The purpose of this class is to become proficient in the life of a mermaid. Upon graduation you will either remain here at the school, help the village to function, or reside at the Queen's kingdom. All of these are important functions of being a mermaid, each just as important as the other."

Surveying the room, her luminous eyes held Simone's for just a second longer than usual. "You and your dragon are very interesting. I would like both of you to stay; however, we must get the Queen's permission because this would be quite an oddity for the school."

"But, when will we know if the Queen will let us attend school?" she asked earnestly.

"Soon, Darling. In the meantime, let's have cookies and get to know each other."

"Hi, my name is Zac," said a fearsome looking barracuda, seated next to Simone. "What is a daydream?"

Trying not to stare at his snake like body and fang-like teeth, Simone answered cautiously. "A daydream is something you think about all the time." She thought Zac, the barracuda, was one of the scariest fish she'd ever seen. Even more so than the Queen herself.

"What do you mean you learned how to travel into a daydream?"

"I travel through a light tunnel driven by a red fox. Why do you ask?"

Zac looked nervously around the room before he whispered, "Because all I think about is becoming a fish that can live on land. I was hoping we could become friends and you would teach me how to do this, so I can come visit your world."

Chapter Ten

Before Simone could answer, Miss Meranda snapped her fingers. "Students, we have news. Mr. Flip has returned with the Queen's ruling."

Nervous chatter filled the classroom as the teacher unfolded the gold scroll of paper. "The Queen says you may stay for mermaid school, but on one condition. The dog-dragon is to become a merman as well, and once school is complete, you must go to her castle together."

"You can't do this to me!" yelled Coop. "I cannot become a merman. Let's go home. I'm calling Wizard right now." He was so upset, he began to stutter. "Thththat is not who I am, it's who the QQQQueen wants me to bbbbe. This is wrong."

"Coop, you are my best friend and this is my biggest dream. You can't back out now," Simone bellowed in fear. Looking anxiously at the teacher, Simone was in tears. "If he becomes a merman, will he have to remain that way?"

"Well, honey, we really won't know that until he completes school and goes through the transformation. But we do know once he is back on land, he will be a Great Dane again. Isn't that enough?"

"No, it's not enough," said Coop as he covered his face with his paws. He thought about bolting from the room, swimming as fast as he could away from this madness. All he had to do was push his black stone and summon Fox.

"I have to go for a swim to think things through. May I please be excused."

"Of course you may, but you only have one hour to decide. After that, it is too late. Think with your heart, dear dragon, not your mind. If you choose not to agree, then no school."

Coop looked miserable as he turned to swim away. "I would rather go to that mean Queen's castle than be a mermaid." he said as he shook Simone off him. She tried desperately to pull him back, but he would not budge. "This is not about you this time, girl. It's about me."

Coop found himself back at the sea sprite cave. He began looking for his little friends, and felt happy for a moment as they zipped around his head. They were so excited as they squealed, "Our friend is back! Look, it's the dragon!"

"Why do you look so sad," asked one of the sprites as she landed on Coop's ear. "You don't like being here?"

"Yes, I really like it here, but the only way my girl can become a mermaid is if I agree to being a merman. That is out of the question."

"Why wouldn't you want to become a merman? That is an important position in our world and would be quite an honor."

"Because, I am a dragon, not a fish. Hey, what's your name?"

"I'm Galatia. I wish I could go to mermaid school. You know, mermaids are just as magical as dragons. There's really no difference except you have two legs and they don't."

Coop just stared at her. *What does a sprite know*, he thought to himself. Nobody understood his dilemma, it seemed.

Galatia danced across his head. "When I turn into a dragonfly, I will still be who I am at heart. All that will change is my appearance. As long as we remain true to ourselves, we can be anything we want to be."

Coop shook his head back and forth sent the little sprite in flight. "All I want to be is a dragon."

Galatia zipped playfully to his face and planted a kiss on top of his big, wet nose. "I think you will be beautiful and strong whether you are a dog, dragon, or merman. You will still be Coop, and that's where the magic lies."

"I have a lot to think about on my swim back. Thank you, Galatia."

Coop thought and thought and thought all the way back to the classroom. When he returned, he had made his decision.

He just hoped nobody would be disappointed in his choice.

Chapter Eleven

Simone threw her arms around his thick neck. "I missed you." He licked her cheek in response and continued swimming to Miss Meranda.

Head held high, posture straight as an arrow, Coop said, "I have made my decision. I will become a merman, but it is important to know if I can change back and forth between dragon and merman."

The pretty teacher stroked his white chest lovingly. "That's the beauty of this. You are a powerful protector already. When you become a merman, you will blend strength with magical powers. You will use all of these blended together only for the good of fellow creatures."

"I'm so proud of you! I love you so much! But, what changed your mind?" Simone hugged him close.

"That's for me to tell on our *next* adventure," Coop had a secretive looking grin on his face.

Miss Meranda smiled as she turned to the class. "I want everyone back here well-rested and ready to learn. We shall begin school at the turn of the tide on the New Moon.

"What do you mean New Moon?" asked Zac the barracuda.

"The magic of the New Moon is that, for one day each month, the Sun and the Moon get together and talk to each other. This is the time for starting new projects, and in our case, school."

She held a moon chart up for everyone to see. "When the Full Moon arrives fourteen days from now, we will learn. After that, we shall take a break until the next New Moon. Any questions?"

"Coop and Simone, since you are going back to land, your time frame is a lot different than ours under sea. You will need to pay close attention to the tides and turn of the moon," said Miss Meranda.

The teacher pulled a beautiful light blue aquamarine crystal from her hair, and handed it to Simone. "This will keep you in touch with the vibrations under the sea and a connection with your new friends here. Safe travels, sweet human."

Simone could not believe she was holding a gift from a mermaid! There was a bright flash of light in the room that distracted her from the aquamarine.

"Your tourmaline is flashing, Coop! That is Wizard telling us it's time to go. Hurry, we have to go! Bye everybody. We will see you at the New Moon!"

The tunnel was waiting for them just outside the Mermaid School cave. Wizard hurriedly ushered them in, then quickly adjusted knobs as they moved toward home. "We'll arrive just in time for dawn. Good job, mates."

Chapter Twelve

Simone yawned and slowly opened her eyes. *"Wow, what a dream I had,"* she thought to herself.

As she rolled over to her side to look at Coop, she felt something hard under her arm. She gasped when it rolled toward her on the sheet. It was a crystal! The aquamarine Miss Meranda had given her!

Leaning off the bed, she examined Coop, who was sleeping soundly and snoring loudly. His collar! It really had stones in it!

Her stuffed fox, Wizard, stared blankly at her from his place on the pillow. She thought he grinned but knew it was just her imagination.

Had they actually gone into her daydream, or was it simply a dream?

"I guess we'll find out at the New Moon," she thought happily as she began to plan, just in case, for mermaid school.

Want to know more about the real life Coop? Go to this link to see a behind-the-scene look at the dog who morphs into a see dragon!

www.crystaljourneyadventures.com